Usborne Farmyard Tales

CURLY TALES

Heather Amery
Illustrated by Stephen Cartwright

Language Consultant: Betty Root

There is a little yellow duck to find on every page

Notes for Parents

Your child will want to share these stories with you many times.

All the *Farmyard Tales* stories have been written in a special way to ensure that young children succeed in their efforts to read.

To help with that success, first read a whole story aloud and talk about the pictures. Then encourage your child to read the short, simpler text at the top of each page and read the longer text at the bottom of the page yourself. This "turn about" reading builds up confidence and children love joining in. It is a great day when they discover they can read all the story for themselves.

These two *Curly Tales* provide an enjoyable opportunity for parents and children to share the excitment of learning to read.

Betty Root

PIG GETS
STUCK

This is Apple Tree Farm.

This is Mrs. Boot, the farmer. She has two children, called Poppy and Sam, and a dog called Rusty.

On the farm there are six pigs.

The pigs live in a pen with a little house.
The smallest pig is called Curly.

It is time for breakfast.

Mrs. Boot gives the pigs their breakfast.
But Curly is so small, he does not get any.

Curly is hungry.

He looks for something else to eat in the pen.
Then he finds a little gap under the wire.

Curly is out.

He squeezes through the gap under the wire.
He is out in the farmyard.

He meets lots of other animals in the farmyard.
Which breakfast would he like to eat?

Curly wants the hens' breakfast.

He thinks the hens' breakfast looks good.
He squeezes through the gap in the fence.

Curly tries it.

The hens' food is so good, he gobbles it all up.
The hens are not pleased.

Mrs. Boot sees Curly.

Curly hears Mrs. Boot shouting at him.
"What are you doing in the hen run, Curly?"

He runs to the fence.

He tries to squeeze through the gap. But he has eaten so much breakfast, he is too fat.

Curly is stuck.

Curly pushes and pushes but he can't move.
He is stuck in the fence.

They all push.

Mrs. Boot, Poppy and Sam all push Curly.
He squeals and squeals. His sides hurt.

Curly is out.

Then, with a grunt, Curly pops through the fence.
"He's out, he's out," shouts Sam.

He is safe now.

Mrs. Boot picks up Curly. "Poor little pig," she says. And she carries him back to the pig pen.

Curly is happy.

"Tomorrow you shall have lots of breakfast," she says. And Curly was never, ever hungry again.

PIG GETS
LOST

This is Apple Tree Farm.

This is Mrs. Boot, the farmer. She has two children, called Poppy and Sam, and a dog called Rusty.

Mrs. Boot has six pigs.

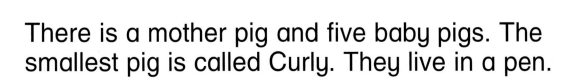

There is a mother pig and five baby pigs. The smallest pig is called Curly. They live in a pen.

Mrs. Boot feeds the pigs every morning.

She takes them two big buckets of food.
But where is Curly? He is not in the pen.

She calls Poppy and Sam.

"Curly's gone," she says. "I need your help to find him."

"Where are you, Curly?"

Poppy and Sam call to Curly. "Let's look in the hen run," says Mrs. Boot. But Curly is not there.

"There he is, in the barn."

"He's in the barn," says Sam. "I can just see his tail." They all run into the barn to catch Curly.

"That's not Curly."

"It's only a piece of rope," says Mrs. Boot. "Not Curly's tail." "Where can he be?" says Poppy.

"Maybe he's eating the cows' food."

But Curly is not with the cows. "Don't worry," says Mrs. Boot. "We'll soon find him."

"Perhaps he's in the garden."

They look for Curly in the garden, but he is not there. "We'll never find him," says Sam.

"Why is Rusty barking?"

Rusty is standing by a ditch. He barks and barks.
"He's trying to tell us something," says Poppy.

"Rusty has found Curly."

They all look in the ditch. Curly has slipped
down into the mud and can't climb out.

"We'll have to lift him out."

"I'll get into the ditch," says Mrs. Boot. "I'm coming too," says Poppy. "And me," says Sam.

Curly is very muddy.

Mrs. Boot picks Curly up but he struggles. Then he slips back into the mud with a splash.

Now everyone is very muddy.

Sam tries to catch Curly but he falls into the mud.
Mrs. Boot grabs Curly and climbs out of the ditch.

They all climb out of the ditch.

"We all need a good bath," says Mrs. Boot.
"Rusty found Curly. Clever dog," says Sam.

First published in 2000 by Usborne Publishing Ltd. Usborne House, 83-85 Saffron Hill, London EC1N 8RT Copyright © Usborne Publishing Ltd. 1989,1990,2000